For Adri, Grace, and Joseph

What This Story Needs Is a Bang and a Clang
Copyright © 2017 by Emma J. Virján. All rights reserved. Manufactured in China. No part of this book may be used or reproduced in any manner whatsoever without written permission except in the case of brief quotations embodied in critical articles and reviews. For information address HarperCollins Children's Books, a division of HarperCollins Publishers, 195 Broadway, New York, NY 10007. www.harpercollinschildrens.com

ISBN 978-0-06-241530-1

The artist used charcoal sketches painted digitally to create the illustrations for this book.
Typography by Dana Fritts
16 17 18 19 20   SCP   10 9 8 7 6 5 4 3 2 1
❖ First Edition

WHAT THIS STORY NEEDS IS
A BANG AND A CLANG

By Emma J. Virján

HARPER
An Imprint of HarperCollinsPublishers

What this story needs is
a pig in a wig,

building a stage,

arranging a stand,

Pig in a

and getting set to conduct the Pig in a Wig Band.

a squeak!

A startle,
a jump,
an EEK, and
a SHRIEK!

What this story needs now is to get back on track.

Mouse wants to play.
Here's my baton.
Let's fix up the stage.
The show must go on!

And now for . . .
a ping,
a brup,
a twang,
and a buzz,

a tish,
a tootle,
a bwap,
and a
boom,

an oompah,
a jingle,
and a doom-
doom-doom.

What this story needs now is . . .